BODY ARTS

THE HISTORY OF TATTOOING AND BODY MODIFICATION™

THE CULTURE OF SCARIFICATION

Monique Vescia

Rosen YA™
New York

Published in 2019 by The Rosen Publishing Group, Inc.
29 East 21st Street, New York, NY 10010

First Edition

Cataloging-in-Publication Data

Names: Vescia, Monique, author.
Title: The culture of scarification / Monique Vescia.
Description: New York : Rosen Publishing, 2019 | Series: Body arts : the history of tattooing and body modification | Includes bibliographical references and index. | Audience: Grades 9–12.
Identifiers: ISBN 9781508180708 (library bound) | ISBN 9781508180715 (pbk.)
Subjects: LCSH: Scarification (Body marking)—Juvenile literature. | Body marking—Juvenile literature. | Body art—Juvenile literature.
Classification: LCC GN419.15 V44 2019 | DDC 391.6'5—dc23

Manufactured in the United States of America

CONTENTS

INTRODUCTION

Human beings are tribal creatures. We remain remarkably loyal to the communities and groups to which we belong, and we often feel actively hostile toward the members of other groups. They may seem strange and alien to us, and sometimes hardly human. Yet any student of history can tell you that over the course of our evolution, humans everywhere have been driven by precisely the same desires as our distant ancestors. One of these is the compulsion to change, augment, and adorn the bodies we were born with.

Body modification has been practiced by every human group, for hundreds of thousands of years. This ancient cultural practice, which now encompasses everything from corset piercings and eyeball tattoos to plastic surgery and breast implants, satisfies a range of human needs, whether aesthetic, spiritual, social, personal, or some combination of the above. Cutting and styling one's hair and body painting rank among the most temporary techniques for modifying the body. Tattoos and piercings represent more of a commitment, but it is possible to erase or reverse the effects of each of these modifications. Among the most permanent are

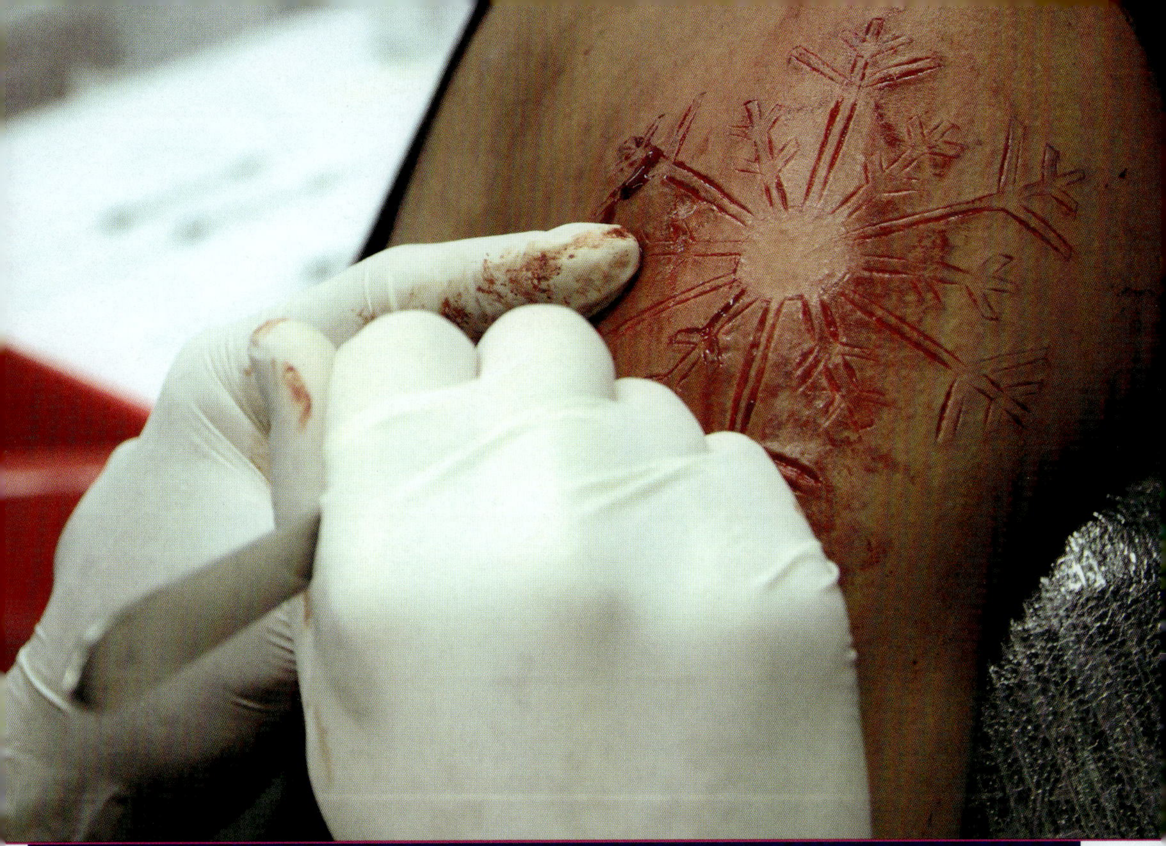

A body artist makes precise cuts with a scalpel to create a snowflake pattern. The wounds will ultimately heal into a decorative scar along the lines of these cuts.

amputation and scarification. These last are the modifications one lives with for life.

Most scars occur by accident, the result of an injury inflicted upon an unwilling subject. Scarification is the practice of intentionally wounding the flesh to create a particular design or pattern of scars as the body heals itself. Historically, people who endured the pain and disfigurement of scarification may not always have done so voluntarily. In some cultures, scarification has been part of traditional coming-of-age rituals, required of every youth at a particular time in their lives. Infants in some African tribes who receive their first scars at the age of a few months do not have a choice.

However, as scarification gradually gains in popularity in today's body modification communities, people who undergo this body art technique do so willingly. They may wish to have a piece of body art that is strikingly unique and unusual, or that feels powerfully rebellious. They may see scarification as a way to memorialize a lost loved one, celebrate their ethnic heritage, or signal their allegiance to a certain group or subculture. Or they may simply believe that scars make the body more interesting.

There is something almost magical about a scar: the body spontaneously stitches together and repairs a wound that might otherwise, in some cases, be fatal. Some people wear their accidental scars as badges of honor, proof of their capacity to recover from life's injuries and to endure. After all, one of the most famous fictional characters of all time, Harry Potter, "the Boy Who Lived," has a scar shaped like a lightning bolt on his forehead.

But the thought of deliberately damaging one's body to create an intentional scar remains profoundly disturbing to many. The expression "scarred for life" has come to mean something more than a permanent physical mark on the surface of the skin. It refers instead to a deep and lasting psychological trauma. Serious scarification practitioners understand that scars are powerful negative symbols. One reason many tattoo and piercing artists feel drawn to this form of body art is for the challenge of transforming something with negative associations into something positive and beautiful. A person who volunteers to have their flesh cut or burned to create a permanent scar must have a powerful motivation for doing so.

CHAPTER 1

AN ANCIENT PRACTICE

Body modification, the deliberate alteration of one's physical appearance or anatomy, is an ancient practice that finds expression in every culture on earth. Some methods of modification, such as hair styling, shaving of body hair, and applying makeup and nail polish, have become so much a part of many people's daily routines that they don't think of these acts as modifications.

Other more permanent body art methods, such as tattooing and piercing, long practiced in other cultures, were once relatively rare in industrialized societies. Today, however, they have become increasingly commonplace. Scarification, also known as cicatrization, is a permanent type of body modification in which designs and patterns are etched or cut into the skin. The resulting scars from this controlled type of injury permanently transform the texture and appearance of the skin's surface.

WRITING ON THE BODY

The Luba people of the Congo region of Africa traditionally use both elaborate hair styling and scarification to create a record of an individual's personal history and his or her place in society. As a man or woman ages, more "information" is added to his or her body. For instance, the shape and color of a hairdo might be altered to signify changes in marital and employment status. The body becomes a book where a person's entire history can be read. The word meaning "to scarify" (*kulemba*) was adopted to mean "to write" once the Luba became literate.

EARLY EVIDENCE

Scarification is among the oldest types of body modification that humans practice. It dates back to the Paleolithic era (8000 BCE), according to evidence found at an archaeological site at Ain Ghazal in present-day Jordan. Two headless figurines of fertility goddess statues were unearthed with curving scarification lines on their abdomens and buttocks. A rock painting from around 7000 BCE also depicts a female deity, in this case a horned goddess, with scarification patterns on her breasts, belly, shoulders, thighs, and calves.

Similar scarification designs as those seen on archaeological finds have been noted on women from

Visitors to a museum in Jordan examine a statuette of a human figure unearthed at Ain Ghazal. Such archaeological finds help people learn about scarification's cultural origins.

Central and West Africa. Scarification also has been practiced in Papua New Guinea, Australia, and South, Central, and North America. Notably, the practice tends to flourish in places where people have so much melanin in their skin that a tattoo would not be very visible.

THE SIGNIFICANCE OF SCARS

The significance of the procedure and the meaning of the scars it creates vary from one culture to the next.

Some scars indicate different stages in a person's life. In Africa's southern Sudan, Nuba girls at the beginning of puberty are marked on their forehead, chest, and abdomen. When they begin to menstruate, they receive a second set of cuts under their breasts. Once their first child has been weaned, they undergo a final elaborate series of scars across the chest, neck, back, buttocks, and legs.

The Ekoi people of southeast Nigeria believe that the scars on their bodies will serve as money on their way to the afterlife. For the Bafia people of Cameroon, scarification is a process of humanization: without scars, a person would be indistinguishable from other animals.

THE TEETH OF THE CROCODILE

In Papua New Guinea, boys as young as eleven undergo scarification as part of an excruciating initiation ritual. The notion that humans evolved from crocodiles is part of the Sepik tribe's creation myth. Wounds sliced into the chest, back, and buttocks with a sliver of bamboo test the initiate's self-control and ability to endure pain. Clay and tree oil are rubbed into the wounds to help the resulting scars resemble scales. The scars represent the teeth marks of the crocodile that "eats" the young man during the month-long ceremony celebrating his passage into manhood.

Some groups use scars as a form of preventative medicine, believing that scars above the eyes can improve the eyesight, and a four-pointed star near the liver will protect against hepatitis. The practice also has a role in healing rituals, where the ability to endure pain is an important part of the experience. Scarification is a bloody procedure, and in most hunting and gathering cultures, people believe that shedding blood can summon the gods as well as good and evil spirits.

Scarification was once widely practiced by Australia's Aboriginal peoples. Around the age of sixteen or seventeen, boys and girls were both marked with long cuts made by a sharpened stone tool. A stick, heated to glowing in a fire, was then used to cauterize the wounds and to encourage scars to form. Different clans displayed different sizes and patterns of scars, which re-created ancestral landscapes like those in Aboriginal body painting. By touching a scar, these people believed they could access a deeper level of consciousness and telepathically communicate with their ancestors.

CHANGING CUSTOMS

In West Africa, where the practice of scarification is dying out, older people still bear the facial scars they received in their youth. The marks were once a way to distinguish between warriors from opposing tribes, as well as a sign of social status and group identity.

This young woman from Burkina Faso, a country in Africa, bears dramatic facial scars that identify her as a member of a specific tribe.

Mien Guemi, a painter from Burkina Faso, has said, "No need for an ID card, I always wear my identity on my face. This is the reason why people did it: to recognize one another." Today, scarification has become socially unacceptable and is prohibited by law in Burkina Faso.

With its long and complex cultural history, body modification will always be a feature of human behavior. But trends in body modification come and go. Modern women don't wear bustles, except as costumes, and people no longer tightly wrap infants' heads to reshape the skull into a conical or wedge shape. But as scarification dies out in many non-Western societies, it has become more common in other places. In many industrialized countries today, young adults have enthusiastically embraced body modifications such as tattoos and piercings. These types of body art, once regarded as transgressive and rebellious, have become relatively mainstream. Individuals looking to express their individuality have sought out body modification practices, such as scarification, that still retain much of their shock value.

This is a newly carved scarification design on a person's abdomen. Over time, these angry-looking cuts will fade and be replaced by a pale pattern of scar tissue.

During the twentieth century, subcultures such as the punks and modern primitives practiced methods of body modification including scarification. Punk, which emerged during the mid-1970s and continues to influence fashion, music, and literature, was antiestablishment and pro individual freedom. Malcolm McLaren, former manager of the punk band the Sex Pistols, once said, punk "made ugliness beautiful." Spiked mohawks, tattered clothing, and safety-pinned faces have become shorthand for punk style today. The "modern primitives" of the late 1980s and early 1990s embraced ancient ritualistic practices such as scarification as part of their rejection of mass culture.

In the twenty-first century, people who practice scarification do so for many of the same reasons that our ancestors did. They may see it as a means of beautifying the body or expressing their individuality, as a test of strength and endurance, or as a deeply spiritual experience that restores their connections to humanity's ancient ways.

CHAPTER 2

ON THE CUTTING EDGE

Scars are more dynamic than tattoos. Unlike inked designs, scars continue to change as a person ages, so that a scarification design will look different at three months, at one year, and at five years. Scars tend to expand, but as they mature, they may get puffier. Over time, the texture or the color may change. This evolution varies from person to person.

A body modification artist creates the design, but an individual's body creates the scar. In this respect, some people feel that their intentional scars truly belong to them in a way that their tattoos do not. A tattoo design can be replicated on any number of people, but a scarification design is as unique as a fingerprint. Because scarification is still considered a type of extreme body art, this method appeals to people looking for something unusual and rare that relatively few individuals have.

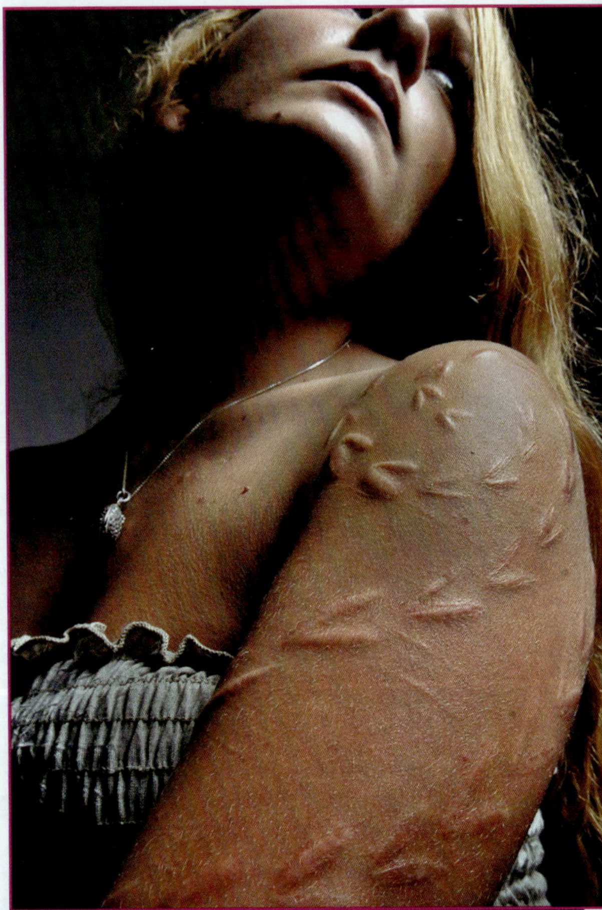

This is a fully healed scarification design. The appearance of the raised scars on this woman's shoulder and arm will continue to change over time.

A potential client must be willing to endure the pain of the procedure. Scarification artists are not licensed to anesthetize their patients, though a topical numbing ointment can be applied before the procedure to help minimize the pain. Cutting techniques of scarification produce a lot of blood and look extremely gory, but some clients claim that the procedure is no more painful than getting a tattoo.

EXPERIENCE COUNTS

All scarification methods come with serious health risks. A reputable scarification practitioner will have plenty of experience in this art form and a long list of satisfied customers willing to provide references. Potential clients should ask to see an album showing photographs of the artist's work that includes examples

SKIN CARVER: PROFILE OF A PRACTITIONER

Scarification artist Ryan Ouellette is one of a relatively small group of people practicing this type of body modification. His first client was himself. When his friends saw the scar pattern he'd carved into the skin of his own leg, they wanted Ryan to create scarification designs for them, too. As he honed his skills, Ryan's clientele grew by word of mouth. Now he even gives talks about scarification at the reputable TED conference.

Ryan began as a professional piercer, and he says that some of his interest in scarification comes from his fascination with human anatomy. He approaches each design as a technical challenge. Unlike a tattoo artist who sees the skin as a blank canvas, Ryan sees the body as layers of skin and various kinds of tissues and blood vessels. He uses scalpels to do all his cuts and takes great care to ensure a sterile environment when working on a client.

of fully healed pieces. Artist reviews online and body art community forums that discuss different artists' work are also a useful resource for clients.

A limited number of people practice this type of body art, and many travel to different areas to work on clients. Body modification shows are a good place to learn about different artists working in the body modification community. People should never trust their skin to someone who doesn't come highly recommended.

IN THE STUDIO

During an initial consultation, the body modification artist will often create a stencil of the desired design and position it on the body so the client can fully visualize the effect that the scar will ultimately create. A skilled artist knows how scars tend to form on different areas of the body and may suggest some revisions in the client's initial design to ensure the best final result. Certain areas of the body are not suited to scarification, such as the belt line, where pressure from clothing will affect the way the scar forms.

Depending on which technique is used and how elaborate the design is, the process can take anywhere from thirty minutes to six hours. During the three-stage process, the scarification artist will first create a shallow outline of the design. Next comes a detailed outline, when the artist creates any thin and thick lines, adds depth to the design, and cleans up the corners. Finally, large areas of skin are removed to create solid sections of scar tissue. For the finished scar to have a consistent look, the entire design must be created in a single session.

TECHNIQUES OF THE TRADE

Some of the oldest methods for producing scars on the body are still in use today. These include cutting and

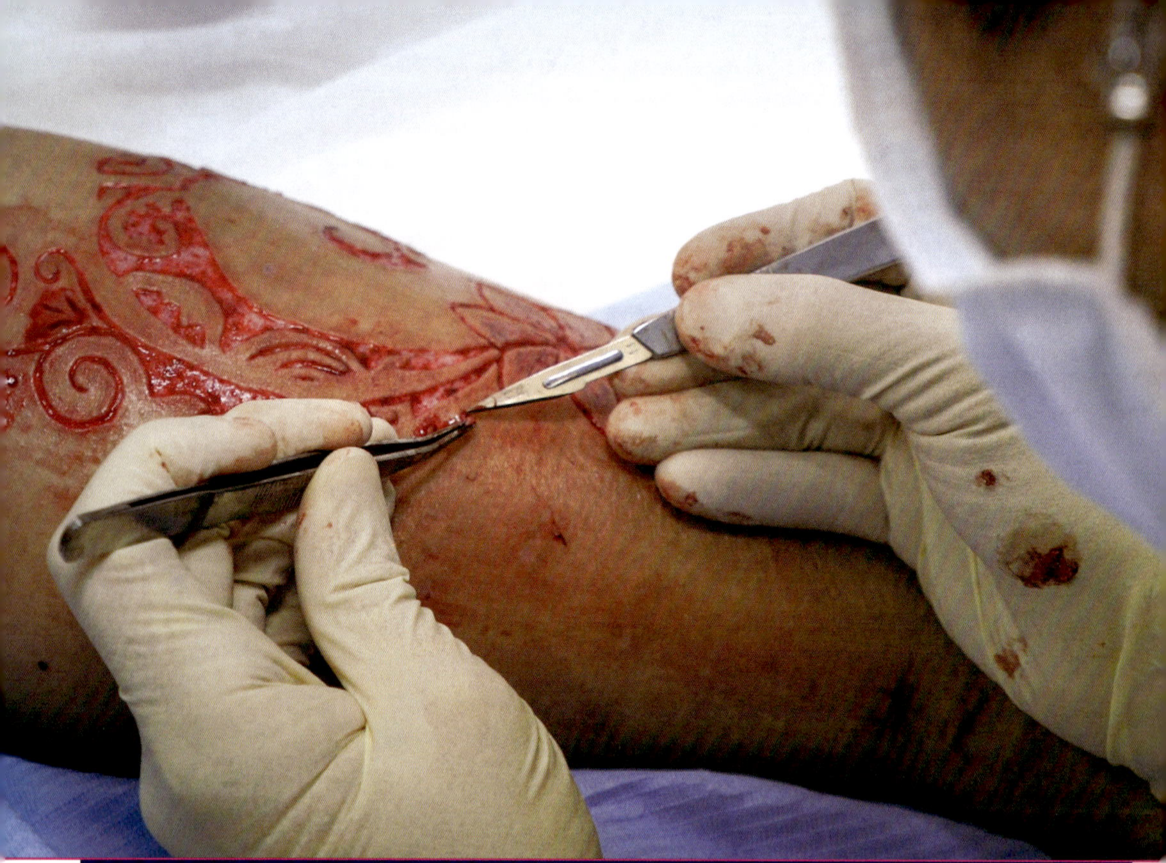

A scarification artist uses a scalpel to etch a design into a customer's leg. The tweezers help lift away patches of peeled skin.

removing the top layers of skin, or rubbing portions of it away. The longer a wound takes to heal, the more prominent the scar will be. Scarification artists use various techniques to inhibit and prolong the healing of the wounds they create.

CUTTING

Some of the earliest tools used to create scars were sharpened pieces of bone. Today, many scarification artists use super-sharp scalpels or surgical blades to cut into the skin.

Some "scarifiers" are single-use disposable blades. Hobby blades such as X-Acto knives are not suitable for this type of work. Duller than a scalpel and slightly serrated, these blades may result in jagged cuts and uneven scarring. In addition, hobby blades are often oiled, which can irritate cuts. Blades must be changed

MEMORIAL SCARIFICATION

People often get a piece of body art to commemorate a lost loved one. They may ask to have a deceased person's name, death date, or portrait tattooed on their body, to serve as a constant reminder of that individual. The pain of the procedure and the permanence of the body art becomes a meaningful way to honor that loss.

Receiving an intentional scar can also be an act of mourning and memorialization. In addition to honoring an individual, some people will enhance a scarification pattern by rubbing the ashes of that person's cremated body into the wound. By doing so, the bereaved person actually incorporates a part of the lost one into their own body. Because scars change the texture of the skin, even touching the design can bring the deceased to mind.

frequently, and an artist may use as many as thirty blades in a single session.

The cuts made in the skin are approximately one-sixteenth of an inch (one-fifth of a centimeter) deep. Shallow cuts don't create fully visible scars, and deeper ones may result in health complications such as nerve damage.

PACKING

One technique used in combination with cutting is called "packing." This method is more common in Africa than the United States and involves packing the wound with clay or ash; in the United States, cigar ashes or even the ashes of a loved one may be used to pack a wound. During healing, the body will push out the packing material, resulting in a larger raised scar.

SKIN REMOVAL, OR SKINNING

Single-line cuts made with a scalpel make thin lines in the skin. To create larger areas of scar tissue, the artist will create an outline with a scalpel and then peel off the skin within the outline. This method may create scars with an uneven texture. Sometimes the skin inside the initial outline is lifted with a tool and inert materials such as clay or ash are packed under the lifted skin, and the wound allowed to heal. The healing process takes quite a while and complications may occur.

HATCHING

Hatching, another technique for removing large areas of skin, is done with a sterile surgical scalpel. It resembles the crosshatching done with a pencil while sketching, but the scarification artist draws the lines through the skin with a scalpel. Hatching takes longer than the skinning method but can be useful for small, detailed designs and creating shading effects.

ABRASION

The abrasion method uses friction to create scarring. Power or Dremel tools tipped with sandpaper, steel wool, or grinding stones can be used by a scarification artist to remove layers of the skin. Abrasion can be done manually as well, as it was originally before power tools became available. This method creates more subtle scars than cutting methods.

TATTOO GUN SCARIFICATION

A scarification artist can create a design by using a tattoo machine without the ink to etch patterns into the skin. Also called etching, this method may be a preferable alternative for someone who would rather not have her or his skin cut or branded. The wound usually heals to leave a faint but detailed scar.

THE HEALING PROCESS

Some artists will fill a finished scarification design with liquid skin adhesive to keep the wound open and create a more visible scar. After the procedure, the bandage applied by the artist must be left in place for twelve hours. Then the bandage should be gently removed and the wound washed with warm water and mild soap and dried gently and thoroughly with a paper towel. No ointments should be applied to the skin, though some people use irritants like toasted sesame oil to intentionally inhibit the healing process.

Once it is washed and dried, the wound must be covered with plastic wrap from a fresh roll (to minimize contamination), then sealed off with medical tape. During the first week of healing, the design must be unwrapped, washed and dried, and rewrapped several times a day. The plastic wrap slows down the healing process to create a more pronounced scar. The person should not swim or soak in a tub during this time, and clean clothes should be worn every day. It's also important not to let anyone's bodily fluids come in contact with the healing wound, since this can lead to infection. Some people choose to abandon the wrapping period early and to allow a scab to form. Picking at this scab can cause uneven scarring and impact the final design.

If a wound is kept clean and properly cared for, initial healing—meaning the wound is fully covered by a new layer of skin—will take from one to two weeks. After initial healing, it takes several months for scar tissue to form. Throughout the healing process, people may experience skin discoloration around the wounds, tenderness, swelling, bruising, and itching. Six to twelve months after the procedure, the scar will be complete.

CHAPTER 3

FIRE AND ICE

While skin removal techniques represent some of the earliest methods of scarification still in use today, scar designs can also be created by burning off the top layers of the skin using a variety of technologies. Extreme heat and cold as well as highly dangerous chemicals have all been used to create intentional scars on the body. As with all forms of scarification, anyone undergoing these methods of modification should be fully aware of the risks involved. They may also want to give serious thought to their own participation in a practice with a very disturbing history.

A SEARING LEGACY

Scarification can be performed with a very hot or cold branding iron. For hot branding, a shaped piece of metal is heated until glowing and then touched briefly to the skin to create a burn. A scar forms as the burned skin

THE MOST PAINFUL MOD OF ALL

Chemical scarification uses a flesh-burning chemical to achieve a scarred pattern. This method does not create a precise design, and controlling the placement of the chemical is very difficult.

Chemical scarification requires a thorough knowledge of chemistry. Acids, bases, and other caustic chemicals should never be used for this purpose because they work far too quickly, and if they aren't removed in time, they can burn too deeply.

To safely remove chemicals from the area, they must be neutralized, which can be difficult to do. Water may only serve to spread a chemical, and one risks seriously burning the rest of the body.

Finally, the slowly increasing pain of the chemical starting to react must be endured long enough (from two to ten minutes) to achieve the desired design. Unlike in branding, which rapidly destroys the nerve endings, a person undergoing chemical branding will feel every excruciating moment of pain.

heals. The word "brand" dates back to the Old English root meaning "to burn."

Hot branding is a method of scarification with a dark and troubling past. In many cultures, slave owners branded slaves, who were considered property, as a mark of ownership. Branding has also served as a

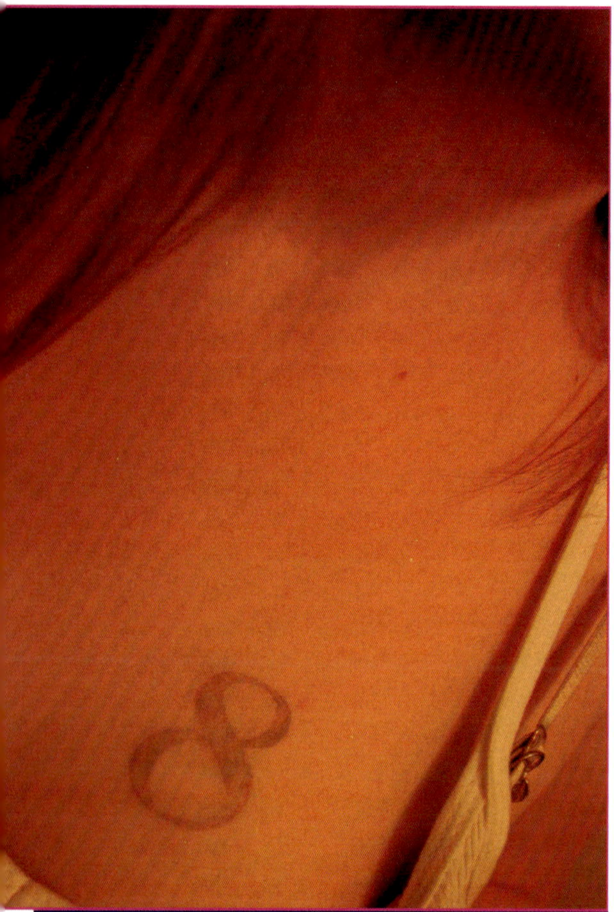

Body branding can be done quickly, though the resulting burn takes a long time to heal. Designs using letters and numbers are called pyrographics.

cruel form of punishment intended to both identify and shame criminals. Ancient Romans branded runaway slaves with the letters *FGV*, which stood for *fugitivus*, and American slaves who attempted escape were branded with an *R* for "runaway."

PLEDGING ALLEGIANCE

Despite these negative associations, branding has become newly popular in body modification communities, though it is one of the riskier methods for producing scars. Members of college fraternities and sororities sometimes volunteer to be branded as part of their initiation rites. (The national councils of these groups strongly oppose the practice, which they denounce as a form of hazing. In some states, such as Indiana, Michigan, and Florida, hazing is a felony.)

Two brothers of the Omega Psi Phi fraternity are branded with Greek letters, signaling their allegiance to that organization. Such brands are rarely created under safe and sterile conditions.

Black fraternities, such as Omega Psi Phi, have been most associated with branding, a practice that may date as far back as the 1930s. A respected member of the fraternity, known as the "hit master," heats a piece of metal (often a coat hanger) bent into the shapes of the fraternity's Greek letters. The initiate's chest or arm will be chilled with ice, or slapped and punched until numb. The red-hot brand is then placed briefly on the skin (the "hit"), creating a second- or third-degree burn.

BAD BEHAVIOR

In 2010, a student at Texas Christian University named Amon Carter IV returned from his winter break with third-degree burns. Members of the Kappa Sigma fraternity and Tri Delta sorority had traveled together to Breckenridge, Colorado, for a ski trip. One night Amon drank enough alcohol to pass out, and he woke up in tremendous pain. While he was unconscious, his fraternity brothers had branded three triangles—the Greek letters for Tri Delta—on his buttock with a heated coat hanger.

Amon required multiple plastic surgeries to repair the damage done to his backside, and his family tried to sue the university, but ultimately the case was dismissed. After reviewing videos taken by the participants, officials determined that Amon had voluntarily submitted to the branding.

The resulting scar will form in the shape of those letters. NBA superstars Michael Jordan and Shaquille O'Neal both have Omega Psi Phi brands on their bodies.

STRIKE BRANDING

Strike branding is the most common and traditional form of branding, often seen in western movies. In cattle branding, a rancher will use one iron to mark an animal's hide with an identifying symbol. Strike branding a design on a human being usually happens in several

The practice of livestock branding dates back to 2700 BCE. Each brand identifies a cow's owner and protects cattle from rustlers (thieves). Cattle brands are registered like trademarks.

stages, or strikes. Small strips of stainless steel are heated and applied to the body in a designated pattern. A branding artist usually has many different sizes and shapes of irons, and will build up the design in stages. A propane torch is often used to heat the metal until it glows red-hot, approximately 500 degrees Fahrenheit (260 degrees Celsius). The brand must be pressed in long enough to burn completely through the first two layers of skin.

Once the brand is complete, the wound will be cleaned, then bandaged and wrapped tight with plastic wrap to slow the healing process. Typically, a brand will heal three or four times as thick as the iron used to make it.

LASER BRANDING

Despite its name, laser branding does not involve a laser. Also called electrosurgical branding, this method uses a handheld tool like an arc welder to burn designs into the flesh. The tool generates electric sparks that vaporize the skin on contact. This method can be used to create precise scarification designs. Laser branding does less damage to the surrounding tissue than strike branding and results in a quicker and less painful process.

CAUTERY BRANDING

Scarification artists sometimes burn small fine-line patterns into the skin using a cautery pen, a handheld medical instrument used to cauterize, or burn, the flesh to control blood loss and prevent infection. This device has some drawbacks: it is not powerful enough to create a lasting scar and tends to overheat.

COLD BRANDING

Far more rare than hot branding, cold or freeze branding uses liquid nitrogen or a freezing solution composed of

5 percent dry ice and 95 percent isopropyl alcohol. The branding iron is bathed in the freezing solution and then pressed against the skin. This type of branding is less likely to cause keloids than strike branding.

HEALING AND AFTERCARE

A brand is a third-degree burn and must be taken care of in order to heal properly. The wound should be kept clean and an antiseptic ointment can be applied, and the wound covered with plastic wrap for the first ten days. During this initial ten-day period, some people add an irritant such as sugar to the antibiotic ointment to inhibit the production of new skin, which will make the final scar more pronounced.

During the healing process, a brand will often bleed and ooze. A brand may take as long as six to twelve months to heal, and the healing time and appearance of the final scar will vary widely from person to person. If a client is unhappy with the final result, the design can be rebranded once the brand has healed completely.

CHAPTER 4

REGULATIONS, RISKS, AND REVERSALS

Scarification is typically practiced by piercing and tattoo artists, and currently no single US federal law exists to regulate this profession. Instead, body art legislation varies from one US state to the next. One general area of agreement concerns age limits: the majority of states prohibit body modification artists from practicing on a minor younger than eighteen years of age. For regulatory purposes, the states of Alabama, Arkansas, Colorado, Illinois, Louisiana, New Mexico, and Washington include scarification under the general category of body art, along with tattoos and piercings. As of 2014, only the US states of Kansas, New Jersey, Oregon, and North Carolina had laws on the books expressly prohibiting scarification.

In addition to state laws, body modification artists are required to follow any established health and safety regulations in the specific counties where they practice their trade. In many states, body modification

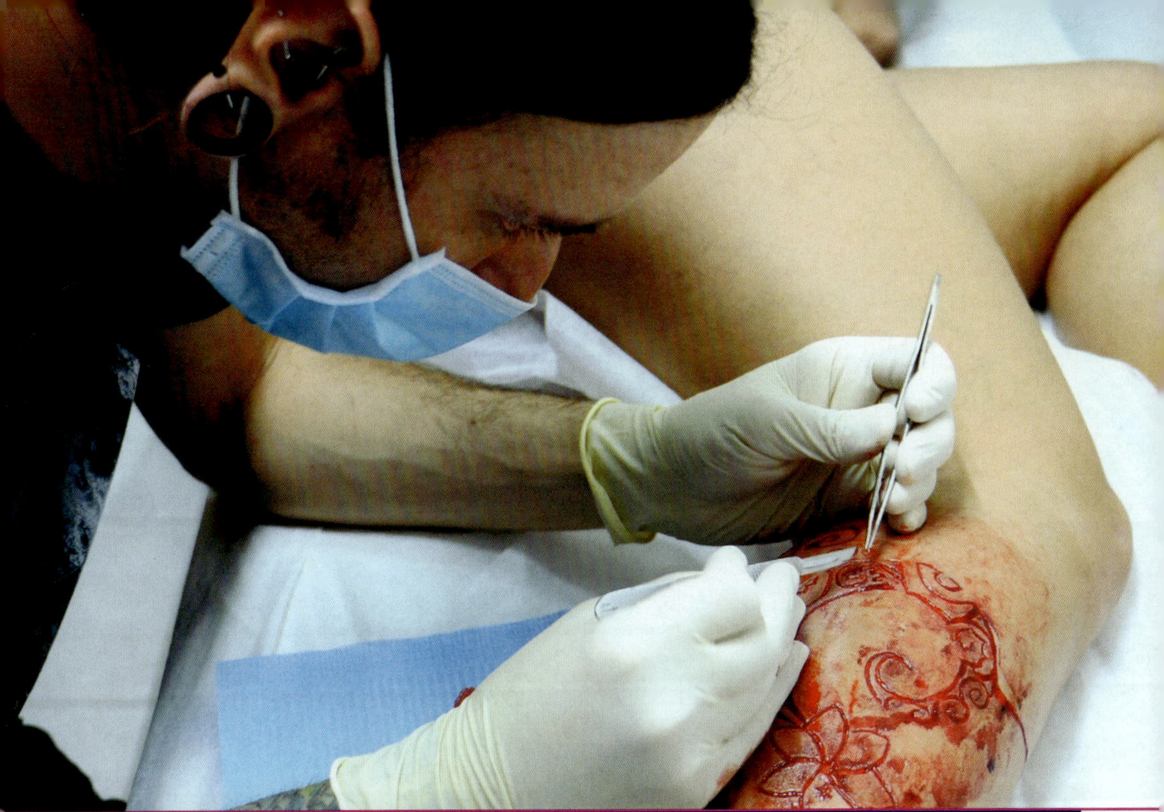

Exposing incised body tissue to the air creates a risk of infection. A face mask and latex gloves help protect both the body artist and his client from blood-borne pathogens.

artists must obtain a special license in order to operate their business, which usually means obtaining a certain amount of training in their field. Artists may be required to take classes in blood-borne pathogens, human anatomy, first aid, and CPR. They may also need to complete a specific number of hours working under the guidance of an experienced practitioner.

In Canada, the Ministry of Health issues guidelines regarding public safety, hygiene, and aftercare that body art practitioners and clients should follow. These guidelines classify scarification and branding as "extreme" body modification procedures and advise that these methods "should be given careful consideration by both client and operator. The enduring physical and psychological impact these treatments may have on the client and those close to them should be taken into account. Procedures may be difficult or impossible to reverse, so the decision to modify the body should not be taken lightly." In 2008, the city of Winnipeg banned any body modifications beyond piercings and tattoos.

The new popularity of these extreme modifications has so far largely outstripped most efforts to regulate them, meaning that practitioners operate in a legal gray area. Since the rules governing these types of body art are open to interpretation, efforts to prosecute scarification artists may prove difficult. Body art practitioners often argue that establishing laws to tightly regulate body modifications will only serve to drive practitioners underground and encourage unskilled artists to operate in secret. This will place body modification clients further at risk.

ADDICTION TO PAIN

Unlike plastic surgeons, body modification artists are not licensed to anesthetize their clients. Anyone who elects to undergo scarification must be psychologically prepared to endure a painful experience, regardless of the technique used. However, many people who choose to modify their body believe that the pain is an

SCARFACE: SCARIFICATION CLIENTS SPEAK

Far more rare than tattoos and piercing, scarification is still considered an extreme body modification. People who volunteer to have designs carved into the skin of their face belong to an even smaller group. Why would anyone agree to this, knowing the procedure is practically impossible to reverse?

Shiva is a scarification artist who has scars on other areas of his body. The practice has profound spiritual meaning for him. He decided to get facial scars because it is "the most sacred part of the body, closest to God." Nevertheless, he advises clients, especially younger ones who do not have many modifications, to reconsider this decision.

Joe got his facial scars on a whim. He'd undergone other modifications and it just "felt like the thing to do." He was working at a bank in London and his employers decided his scars didn't meet the company dress code. Joe lost his job.

essential part of the process. For some, the trauma of pain becomes a spiritual experience; for others, enduring extreme pain is a form of machismo and a way to prove their mental endurance. Finally, people's ability to tolerate pain varies widely.

Whether a scar is achieved through cutting techniques or by branding, a person undergoing scarification will experience a considerable degree of pain. In response

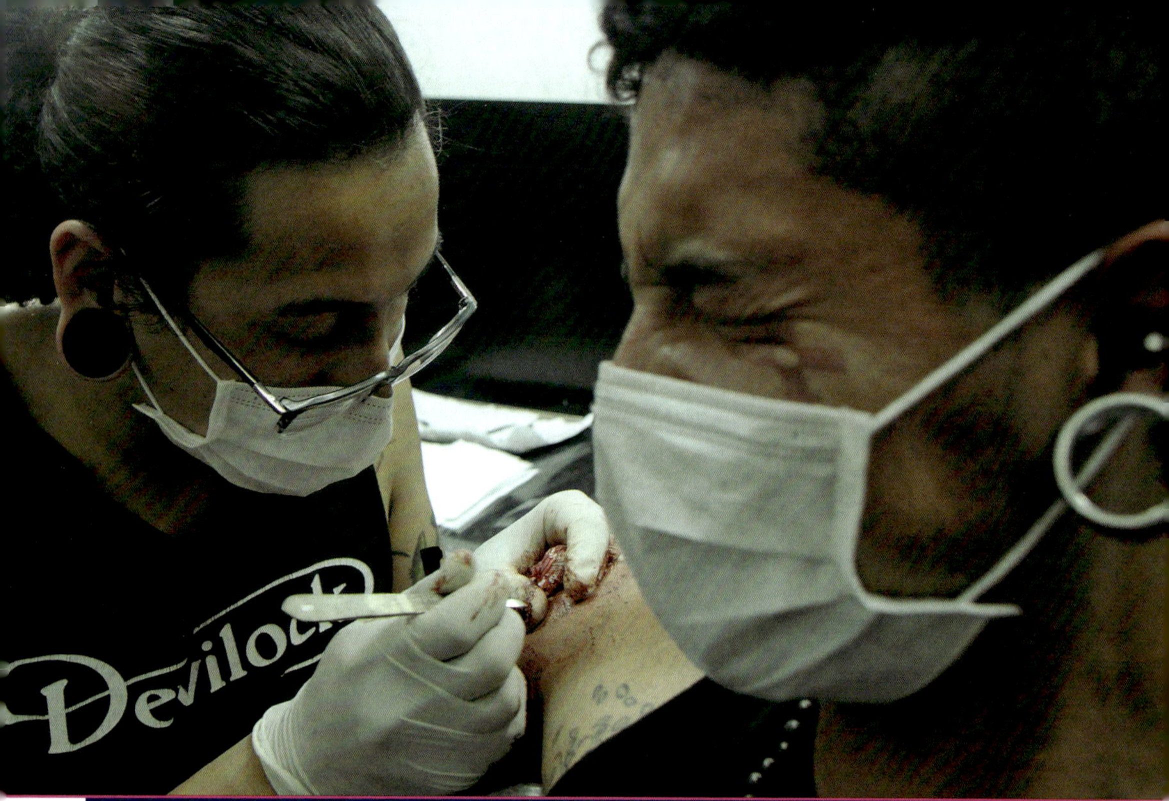

Extreme pain is an unavoidable part of the scarification procedure. Here, a body artist carves an intricate pattern into the skin of a man's arm.

to pain, the body's pituitary gland releases endorphins, which communicate with opiate receptors in the brain. Endorphins reduce our perception of pain in a manner similar to the effects of drugs such as morphine or codeine. After a rush of endorphins, some people may experience euphoria and what is sometimes called a runner's high. For some individuals, the feeling may prove addicting. Endorphins may help explain why an individual compulsively seeks out painful experiences such as body modification procedures. However, an endorphin rush may cause others to become overwhelmed or even pass out.

INFECTION

The skin has an important function in maintaining the body's health: it is a protective barrier against microorganisms. Scarification injures and traumatizes the skin, and this can lead to complications such as infections. Anyone undergoing this procedure should be in good health. Alcohol, nicotine, excessive amounts of caffeine, and illegal drugs can negatively affect the scarification process.

Skilled and conscientious body artists try to create the cleanest possible environment in which to work. The scarification tools must be sterilized in an autoclave, a high-temperature steamer that kills blood-borne pathogens and bacteria. The artist wears latex gloves and a mask. A client's skin must be cleaned—not only in the area where the design will be placed but also in any nearby areas that might come into contact with the wound.

Signs of inflection include a discharge of thick, yellowish pus, red streaks radiating from the wound, skin that feels hot to the touch, and fever. Anyone suffering from infection should see a doctor right away and may be prescribed a course of antibiotics.

BLOOD-BORNE DISEASES

Cutting techniques of scarification are gory procedures, generating far more blood than a tattoo. With the presence of blood comes the potential for contracting a blood-borne infection, for both the client and the artist. Blood-borne pathogens are microorganisms that cause diseases such as HIV/AIDS, and hepatitis B and C. If a scalpel has been previously used on a person infected with a disease and then not properly sterilized, pathogens can be transferred to the next client. HIV is a mutating retrovirus that attacks the human immune system, leading to acquired immune deficiency syndrome, or AIDS. While the symptoms of AIDS can be treated, no known cure currently exists for this disease. Hepatitis B may lead to liver cancer, liver failure, and death. Hepatitis C is a viral infection in the liver that may result in fatal liver disease. As with AIDS, both types of hepatitis can be treated but not cured.

Conscientious scarification artists can drastically reduce risks for themselves and their clients by maintaining a sanitary work environment, disinfecting all work surfaces, sterilizing their tools, wearing masks and latex gloves during the procedure, and properly disposing of bloody blades, bandages, and other biohazards.

KELOIDS

The desired result of scarification is a pattern of raised (hypertrophic) scars that closely follow the design carved in the skin.

Hypertrophic scars heal along the lines of the original wounds and are close to the color of a person's skin. Raised scars create texture on the skin's surface and can add to the appeal of a scarification design. Practitioners sometimes refer to this effect as "keloiding." However, true keloid scars may grow out of control, resulting in lumpy purplish-red masses that destroy the design. A dermatologist can remove them by freezing or burning techniques or with surgery. The tendency to develop keloids is often related to the amount of melanin in a person's skin. People prone to keloids, or who have family members who have developed them, should avoid scarification.

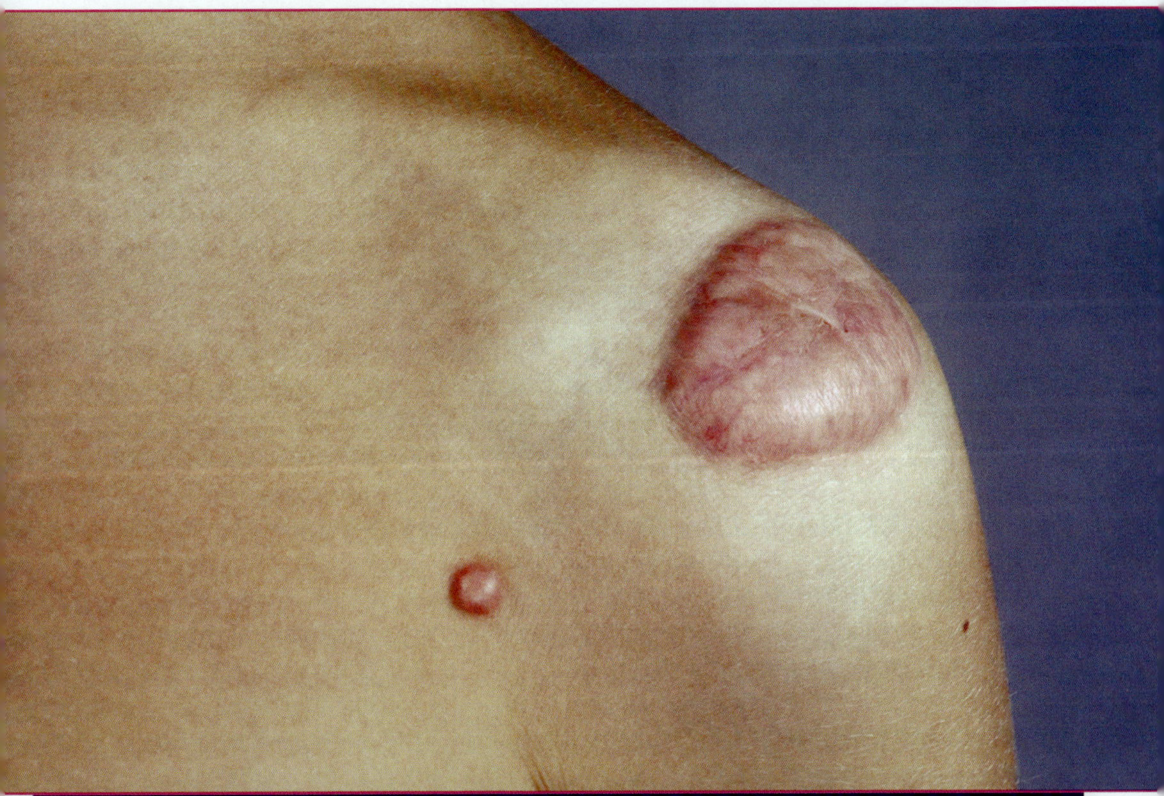

A keloid grows beyond the boundary of the original scar and may be itchy or painful to the touch. It consists of a mass of collagen, a fibrous protein.

SPECIFIC RISKS OF BODY BRANDING

As with all forms of body modification, branding should only be done by someone with plenty of experience in this method. A branding iron pressed too long on the skin can cause nerve damage. Because a brand breaks the skin barrier, it carries a high risk of infection. Precautions to prevent infection include keeping a hygienic workspace, sterilizing equipment after each use, and using disposable single-use tools and materials.

Plenty of do-it-yourself branding videos exist on the internet, but anyone who lets a friend brand them with a heated coat hanger is taking a huge risk. In addition to the dangers posed by infected third-degree burns, the coating on a wire hanger used for branding can flake off, leaving potentially toxic material behind in the wound. Removal of this dangerous metal from the body may require painful surgery. Other health risks related to body branding include allergic reactions and the transmission of other surface infections of the skin, such as staph, tetanus, tuberculosis, fungal infections, and the herpes simplex virus.

HOW PERMANENT IS PERMANENT?

Regardless of the method used, once a scarification wound is made, the body itself controls what the final scar will look like. Even a skilled body artist cannot predict how a particular scar will form or spread. The scar continues to change as the body ages.

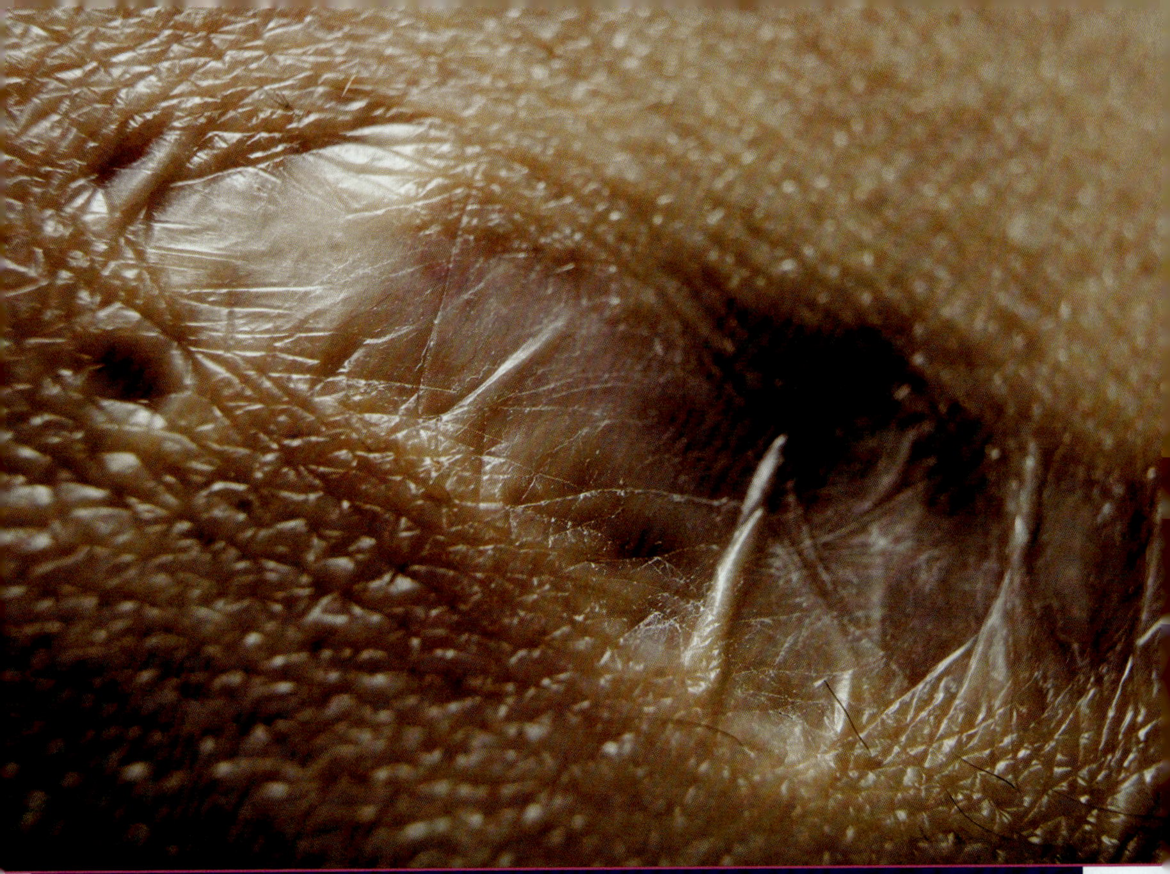

Scar formation can be highly unpredictable. If a client is unhappy with the final appearance of an intentional scar, he or she may have to live with it.

A scar created by branding cannot be reversed. A cosmetic operation will not remove a brand entirely, and it cannot be tattooed over. Scarification designs created by skin removal are very difficult to erase. The process requires a skin graft, an expensive and complicated procedure in which healthy skin is removed from one unmarked area of the body and transplanted to another site. Skin grafts can leave a person looking more disfigured than the original scarification did.

CHAPTER 5

MODERN PRIMITIVES

Nearly all methods of body modification practiced today have ancient roots. Scarification is an even older technique than tattooing. To create patterns on their skin, our distant ancestors needed only some type of sharp scratching or cutting implement and the scarring function of the body itself. For some who choose to undergo scarification today, the deep history of the practice is a significant part of its appeal.

RESTORING RITUALS AND STAYING RELEVANT

Fakir Musafar (born Roland Loomis of South Dakota), the so-called father of the modern primitive movement, helped generate renewed interest in body modification in Western culture. In a world increasingly dominated by mass culture, knowledge kept alive by tribal cultures, and passed down from one generation to the next, is being lost. Beginning in the late 1980s, modern primitives

For decades, Fakir Musafar has experimented with and taught many different body modification techniques, including scarification, extreme body piercing, and tattooing. He calls his explorations body play.

sought to revive indigenous body rituals from around the world. This "neo-tribal" movement aimed to reconnect with these ancient rites in order to have a more authentic or spiritual human experience.

During the mid-eighties, as part of this new body modification movement, scarification was first embraced by gay and lesbian subcultures. During the nineties, the modern primitives adopted the practice, and interest in scarification spread across North America to Europe and Australia.

All meaningful art forms must continue to evolve in order to remain relevant. The same is true for body art. Scarification artists have taken an ancient practice and developed new techniques and methods in order to push the boundaries of this art form. They will often try out new and innovative methods by first experimenting on their own bodies and on the skin of willing friends. Some of these new techniques come from collaborations with other talented artists in the body modification community.

COMBINING SCARS AND TATTOOS

Swiss-born body modification artist Yann Brenyak has a lifetime commitment to transforming the body he was born with. "Changing my body has been a desire deep inside me for my entire life," he has said. "It's always been exciting to me that you can alter your body however you'd like and make fantasy a reality." Brenyak's body is covered in black tattoos, he has stretched earlobes and microdermal implants in his face, and his tongue forks like a lizard's.

Always driven to push the envelope of his chosen art form, Brenyak began experimenting on his own body with a technique known as "graphic skin removal." This part-tattoo, part-surgical-scarring method results in ghostly looking portraits that seem to stare out from a person's flesh. Brenyak creates these portraits on skin that has been heavily tattooed with black ink. Then he uses a scalpel to carve away thin lines of flesh to create

INK RUBBING

An ink rubbing is when tattoo ink is rubbed into the wounds of a fresh scarification cutting. Different colors of ink can be selectively rubbed into different parts of the design. Sometimes ashes are used in place of tattoo ink for this technique. Artists have also rubbed ultraviolet (UV) ink into scarification cuttings to create scars that glow under a black light.

To make sure the ink stays put, it is essential that it be fully encapsulated within the forming scar tissue. This means that the scabs that form over the scarification wound should not be picked at. Due to the unpredictable nature of the developing scar, the final result of an ink rubbing may be disappointing, like a badly done tattoo.

the image. The resulting scars will show up as white lines etched against the black. The laborious process may take as long as seven hours to complete.

Brenyak also practices other body modification techniques, such as tongue splitting, or bifurcation, and repairing stretched earlobes. He prefers not to do body branding because he finds the smell of burned flesh too unpleasant. Brenyak travels to different body art studios around the world to demonstrate his techniques.

Yann Brenyak is not the only body modification artist experimenting with scar-and-tattoo combinations. People sometimes get a tattoo to cover up or embellish an accidental or unwanted scar. For instance, women have had garlands of flowers tattooed over C-section or tummy tuck scars on their lower abdomens. A person whose intentional scar has lost some of its definition over time may opt to get a tattoo over the scarring to bring the design to life again. Others may plan a modification that takes advantage of the strengths of each body art technique, combined in one unique design. The raised patterns created by scarification can add depth, texture, and interest to a tattoo.

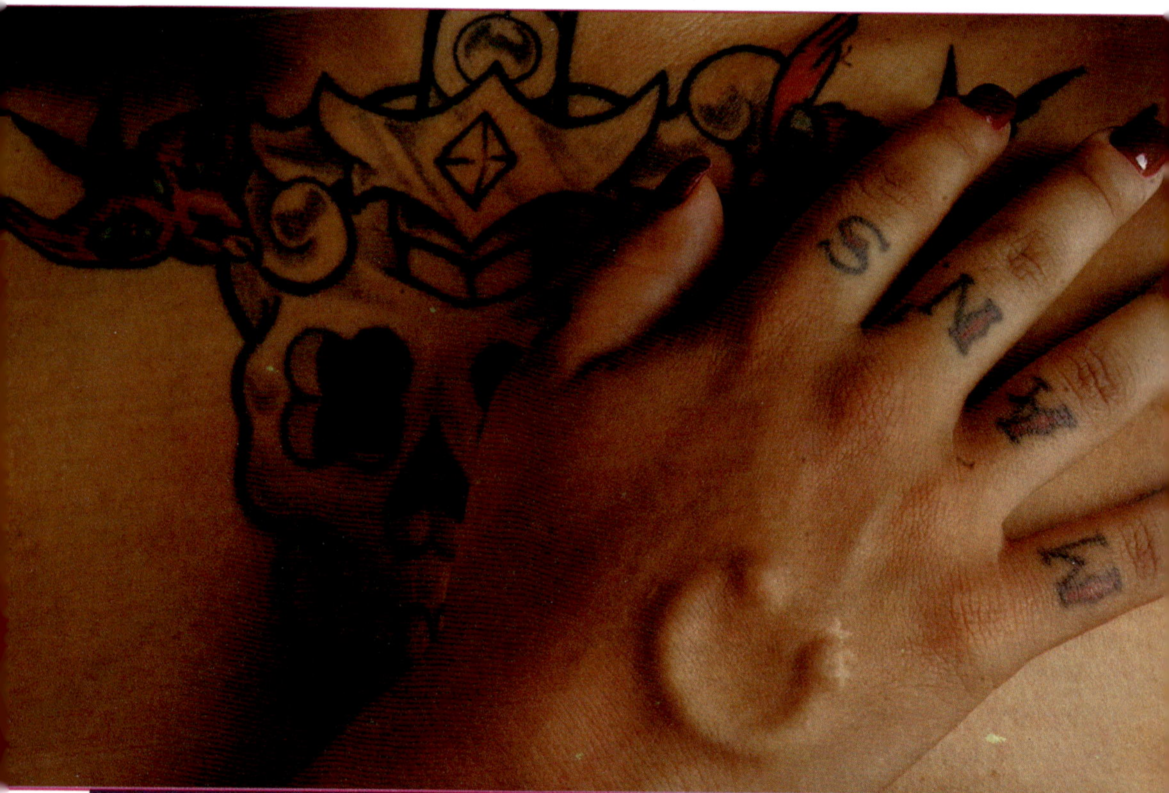

People pushing the boundaries of body modification have gone beyond tattoos and piercing to embrace hardcore mods, such as scarification and implants (shown here in the hand).

ARTISTIC COLLABORATIONS

Sometimes, body modification practitioners with different talents team up to collaborate on a single design. An artist may possess excellent technical skills but not be particularly good at coming up with creative ideas for designs. By working with another artist known for her or his artistic abilities, in combination they can achieve a piece of body art as perfectly executed as it is beautiful.

Body-modification artist Steve Haworth, sometimes known as "the Modfather," is best known for his pioneering work in body art implants, though he also practices

WHERE THE SCARS ARE

In 1977, the first International Tattoo Convention was held in Reno, Nevada. Today, body art conventions held annually all over the world bring together people in the body modification community. These events provide opportunities for artists to showcase their work and for attendees to show off their mods. Featured artists may be local or travel from afar to participate in the event, giving fans a chance to get a piece of body art from an artist who normally practices in another state or country. Expos such as ScarCon and Tattoo Wars are typically three-day affairs that feature live body art demonstrations, tattoo and piercing contests, related merchandise, food, and live music.

other types of body modification. Haworth implants solid silicone body jewelry under the skin to produce startling 3D effects. Haworth has collaborated with artist Wayde Dunn to create complex designs that combine implants with skin-removal scarification and cautery branding.

WHAT'S NEW, WHAT'S NEXT?

Permanent body art techniques such as implants, tongue bifurcation, and scarification are still regarded as hard-core or extreme modifications, practiced by a relatively

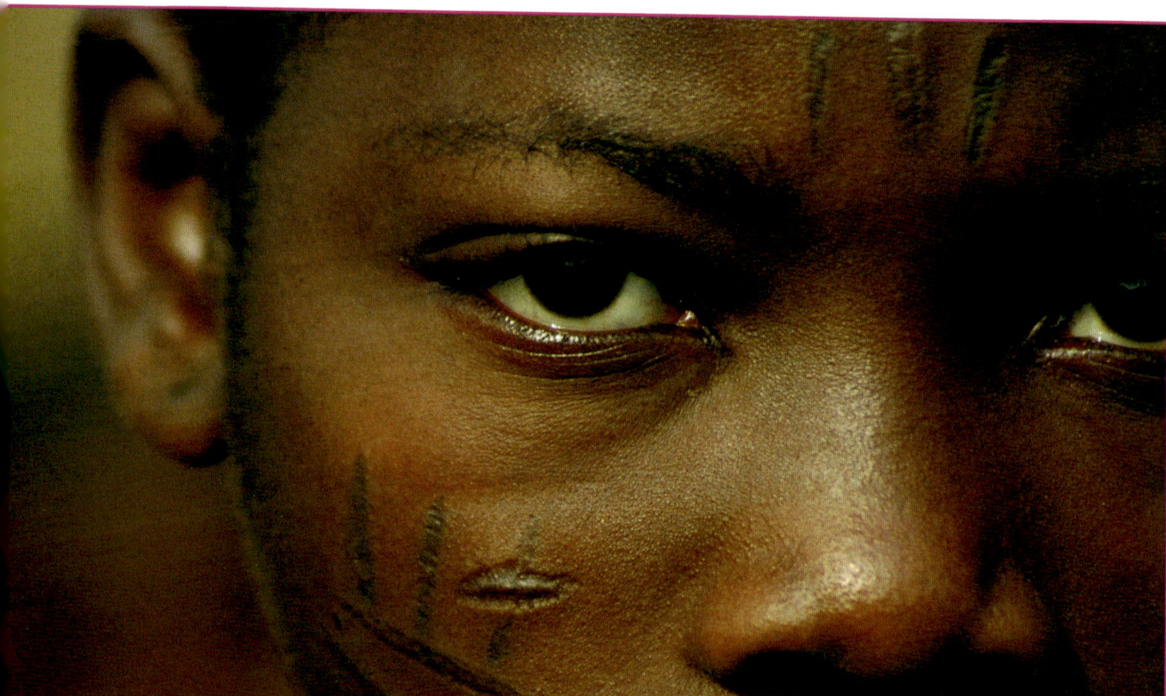

Facial scars such as these on a girl from Benin have a deep cultural significance. While people in North America are just discovering scarification, the practice is declining in Africa.

small group of people. But in the United States, Canada, and other industrialized countries, social attitudes toward other body modification continue to change.

Once regarded as radical, sleeve tattoos and eyebrow and tongue piercings have become mainstream. It's possible to imagine that scarification designs may one day be as common as tattoos and piercings. In the not-too-distant future, the sight of a full facial scar may no longer have the power to shock and unnerve. As long as people still value what is unique and rare, committed body modifiers will always be searching for even more unusual techniques and methods for transforming their own bodies into works of art.

GLOSSARY

ANATOMY The bodily structure of an organism, such as a human or animal.

AUTOCLAVE An apparatus for sterilizing that uses superheated steam under high pressure.

BIFURCATION The division of something into two branches or parts.

BIOHAZARD A risk to human health or the environment.

BLOOD-BORNE PATHOGEN A bacterium, virus, or other microorganism carried in the blood that can cause disease.

BODY ART One of the earliest forms of artistic expression, body art is art made on, with, or consisting of the human body.

BODY MODIFICATION Deliberate altering of the human anatomy or physical appearance, which may include tattooing, piercing, implants, and scarification, as well as cosmetics and hairstyling.

CAUTERIZE To burn the skin of a wound with a heated instrument, typically to stop bleeding.

CICATRIZATION Scar formation at the site of a healing wound.

ENDORPHINS A group of hormones excreted within the brain and nervous system. They activate the body's opiate receptors, dulling the experience of pain.

HARDCORE The most active, committed members of a group or movement.

HYPERTROPHIC SCAR A raised scar resulting from the body's production of collagen.

IMPLANT Something implanted in body tissue. A body-art implant is a substance surgically inserted under the skin to create a 3D effect.

INDIGENOUS Originating or occurring naturally in a particular place; native.

KELOID A thick scar resulting from excessive growth of fibrous tissue.

MELANIN A dark brown to black pigment in the skin. Melanin causes tanning of skin exposed to sunlight.

MICRODERMAL A type of body-art implant that resembles a piercing.

MODERN PRIMITIVE Describing people in developed nations who engage in body modification practices while making reference to the rituals of so-called "primitive" cultures.

SCALPEL A knife with a small, sharp blade.

SKIN GRAFT A surgical operation in which a piece of healthy skin is transplanted to a new site in the body.

STERILIZATION The complete destruction of all microbial life, including bacteria, viruses, and fungi.

SUBCULTURE A cultural group within a larger culture, often having beliefs or interests at variance with the larger culture.

TRANSGRESSIVE Violating accepted or imposed boundaries, especially those imposed by society.

For More Information

Alliance of Professional Tattooists
22025 W. 66th Street
Shawnee, KS 66226
(816) 979-1300
Website: http://www.safe-tattoos.com
This professional group is dedicated to the health and safety issues facing the growing national tattoo industry, including piercing-related concerns.

Body Art Expo
3129 S. Hacienda Boulevard, #322
Hacienda Heights, CA 91745
(626) 961-6522
Website: http://bodyartexpo.com
Body Art Expo is the world's largest tattoo and body art convention, hosting over one hundred body modification artists per show.

Canadian Medical Association
1867 Alta Vista Drive
Ottawa, ON K1G 5W8
Canada
(613) 731-8610 or (800) 663-7336
Website: https://www.cma.ca
This national, voluntary association of physicians publishes a medical journal, featuring several stories published on health issues related to piercings.

Centers for Disease Control and Prevention (CDC) National Institute for Occupational Safety and Health (NIOSH)
1600 Clifton Road
Atlanta, GA 30333
(404) 639-3311
Website: http://www.cdc.gov
The leading federal agency dedicated to protecting the nation's health, the CDC educates the public on the health risks of various body art practices for both clients and artists and how to minimize them. NIOSH promotes productive workplaces and issues information about risks associated with blood-borne pathogens in the body art industry.

University of Pennsylvania Museum of Archaeology and Anthropology
"A World Tour of Body Modification"
3260 South Street
Philadelphia, PA 19104
(215) 898-4000
Website: https://www.penn.museum
Founded in 1887, the museum is the largest university museum in the United States and one of the world's great archaeology and anthropology research museums. The museum's website provides a guided tour through objects in its collection related to body art.

For Further Reading

Beckwith, Carol, and Angela Fisher. *Painted Bodies: African Body Painting, Tattoos, and Scarification.* New York, NY: Rizzoli International Publications, 2017.

Bliss, John. *Preening, Painting, and Piercing: Body Art* (Culture in Action). Chicago, IL: Raintree, 2011.

Camphausen, Rufus C. *Return of the Tribal: A Celebration of Body Adornment.* Rochester, VT: Park Street Press, 1997.

Cohen, Robert. *Body Piercing and Tattooing.* New York, NY: Rosen Publishing, 2013.

Currie-McGhee, Leanne. *Tattoos, Body Piercings, and Teens.* San Diego, CA: Referencepoint Press, 2013.

Krutak, Lars. *Spiritual Skin: Magical Tattoos and Scarification*. Berlin, Germany: Edition Reuss, 2012.

Mercury, Maureen, with photographs by Steve Haworth. *Pagan Fleshworks: The Alchemy of Body Modification*. Rochester, VT: Park Street Press, 2000.

Miller, Jean-Chris. *The Body Art Book: A Complete, Illustrated Guide to Tattoos, Piercings, and Other Body Modifications*. New York, NY: Berkely, 2004.

Rainier, Chris. *Ancient Marks: The Sacred Origins of Tattoos and Body Markings.* New York, NY: Earth Aware Editions, 2006.

Vale, V., ed. *Modern Primitives* (20th anniversary ed.). San Francisco, CA: RE/Search Publications, 2010.

BIBLIOGRAPHY

Barnes, Mo. "Black Fraternity Brothers and the Choice to Brand." Rollingout.com. November 21, 2014. http://rollingout.com/2014/11/21/black-fraternities-choice-brand.

BME Encyclopedia. "Scarification." BMEzine.com. April 5, 2010. https://wiki.bme.com/index.php?title=Scarification.

BME Encyclopedia. "Strike Branding." BMEzine.com. September 8, 2011. https://wiki.bme.com/index.php?title=Strike_Branding.

Brooks, Katherine. "This Is the Last Generation of Scarification in Africa." *Huffington Post*, September 23, 2014. https://www.huffingtonpost.com/2014/09/23/scarification_n_5850882.html.

Cheer, Louise. "Agonising Rites of the Croc Men." *Daily Mail Australia,* August 12, 2014. http://www.dailymail.co.uk/news/article-2722740/The-ancient-initiation-ritual-scars-boys-look-like-crocodiles.html.

The Conversation. "Is Body Branding Legal?" July 28, 2015. https://theconversation.com/the-new-tattoo-is-body-branding-legal-44690.

Denette, Nathan. "People Paying to Have Their Skin Cut, Etched, Burned or Branded as Scarification Gains Popularity." *National Post,* October 14, 2013. http://nationalpost.com/news/canada/people-paying-to-have-their-skin-cut-etched-burned-or-branded-as-scarification-gains-popularity.

Favazza, Armando, MD. *Bodies Under Siege: Self-mutilation, Nonsuicidal Self-injury, and Body Modification in Culture and Psychiatry*. 3rd ed. Baltimore, MD: Johns Hopkins University Press, 2011.

Goldman, Amy. “A Scarification Artist and His Client Talk About the Growing Appeal of Scarification.” *Hellion*, October 13, 2015. http://www.hellionmag.com.

Guynup, Sharon. “Ancient Body Art Leaving New Marks.” National Geographic News, July 28, 2004. https://news.nationalgeographic.com/news/2004/07/0728_040728_tvtabooscars.html.

Kadhim, Lulu. “Why These People Go Through Agony to Intentionally Scar Their Faces.” Vice.com. November 18, 2016. https://www.vice.com/en_us/article/9b8qaz/facial-scarification-interviews.

Laura. “Scarification Aftercare.” Painfulpleasures.com. March 1, 2015. https://info.painfulpleasures.com/help-center/information-center/scarification-aftercare.

Layton, Julia. “How Body Branding Works.” Howstuffworks.com. April 16, 2013. https://people.howstuffworks.com/-body-branding3.htm.

Netter, Sarah. “Texas Fraternity Brother Branded; Family Furious Over Ritual.” ABC News. January 29, 2010. http://abcnews.go.com/WN/texas-fraternity-brother-branded-family-furious-ritual/story?id=9688654.

Network for Public Health Law. State Regulation of Scarification. February 14, 2014. https://www.networkforphl.org/_asset/vgntsm/State_Scarification_Laws_Summary.pdf.

Ouellette, Ryan. "The Intentional Scar." TED talk given at TED X, New England College, January 27, 2015. https://www.youtube.com/watch?v=qCvBCKNStwQ&feature=youtu.be.

Pitt Rivers Museum. "Scarification." 2011. http://web.prm.ox.ac.uk/bodyarts/index.php/permanent-body-arts/scarification.html.

Ronca, Debra. "Can Body Modifications Be Addicting?" Howstuffworks.com. April 13, 2015. https://health.howstuffworks.com/mental-health/can-body-modifications-be-addictive.htm.

Skelton, Jessica. "Beautiful Scars: An Extreme Form of Body Modification." Sheaf, November 3, 2010. http://thesheaf.com/2010/11/03/beautiful-scars-an-extreme-form-of-body-modification.

Skin Artists. "Body Branding." Accessed October 21, 2017. http://www.skin-artists.com/body-branding.htm.

Thomas, Nicholas. *Body Art* (World of Art). London, UK: Thames & Hudson, 2014.

Index

ABOUT THE AUTHOR

Monique Vescia is the author of numerous nonfiction books for young people on a wide range of subjects. Her books include *The Culture of Body Implants*, *Mahatma Gandhi: Champion of the Indian Independence Movement*, *Scientists at Work: Engineers*, *What Is Animal Behavior?* and *The Rise and Fall of the Byzantine Empire*. She makes her home in Seattle, Washington.

PHOTO CREDITS

Cover, p. 1 Marka/Universal Images Group/Getty Images; pp. 5, 38 Juan Cevallos/AFP/Getty Images; p. 10 Kumar Sriskandan /Alamy Stock Photo; p. 13 Thomas S. England/Science Source /Getty Images; p. 14 Eider Manson/EyeEm/Getty Images; p. 17 Al Campanie/Syracuse Newspaper/The Image Works; pp. 20, 35 hafakot/Shutterstock.com; p. 28 Rachel Haller/flickr .com/photos/rachel-amarette/673856721/in/photolist-2/CC BY 2.0; p. 29 The Washington Post/Getty Images; p. 31 FlyBMW /Shutterstock.com; p. 41 BioPhoto Associates/Science Source /Getty Images; p. 43 WIN-Initiative/Neleman/Getty Images; p. 45 Lesv/Wikimedia Commons/FakirMusafar.jpg/CC BY-SA 3.0; p. 48 Craig F. Walker/Denver Post/Getty Images; p. 50 Anthony Asael/Art in All of Us/Corbis News/Getty Images; cover and interior pages Liubomyr Feshchyn/Hemera /Thinkstock (splatters), Gollfx/Shutterstock.com (tattoo design).

Design: Brian Garvey; Layout: Ellina Litmanovich; Photo Researcher: Nicole Baker